Salty Splashes

COLLECTION™

Salty Splashes

COLLECTION™

Salty Splashes

C O L L E C T I O N™

Dreamy Drums

TROUBLE IN PARADISE

JZ Bingham

Illustrations by Curt Walstead

Balcony 7 Media and Publishing

SANTA BARBARA, CALIFORNIA

Balcony 7 Media and Publishing

Printed in the United States of America

ISBN: 978-0-9855453-6-9
Library of Congress Control Number: 2012917872

Additional copies of this book, including bulk orders are
available at www.balcony7.com

Published by Balcony 7 Media and Publishing LLC
133 East De La Guerra St., #177
Santa Barbara, CA 93101
(805) 679-1821
info@balcony7.com
www.balcony7.com

Printed by Lehigh Phoenix

Book Design and Production by DesignForBooks.com
Art Direction, Character and Storyboard Development: Balcony 7 Studios
Cover Art and Interior Illustrations: Curt Walstead

To Samira,

One beautiful name.

Two beautiful souls.

Salty Splashes
COLLECTION™

www.saltysplashes.com

Follow, Share, Visit And Connect With Us
Learn About The Excitement

Also by J.Z. Bingham

Isle of Mystery, Eyes of the King

Gansevort, The King And His Court

A Salty Splashes Collection™

Introduction

Welcome to the *Salty Splashes Collection*™, a world of illustrated fiction for children. *Salty Splashes* tales are told in playful rhymes which are lots of fun to read by kids, as well as adults. Meet our lovable cartoon cast: a precocious bunch who seem to find trouble wherever they go; but they always stick together and learn important lessons along the way. You can meet new characters in every story and join in their antics and adventure. *Salty Splashes* books are in a numbered series but can be enjoyed in any order.

Children of all ages will love these stories because the colorful, detailed illustrations describe every scene and make learning words easier and more exciting.

A balance of easy and more difficult words will help kids expand their vocabulary. Story time is more fun with our mix of narrative and character dialogue because kids can engage in role play, all in rhyme.

Dreamy Drums, Trouble in Paradise is the first book in the *Salty Splashes Collection*™. It introduces our cartoon characters and their sunny, unconventional world. The storyboard designs of Balcony 7 Studios, combined with the hand-drawn illustrations of Curt Walstead, help bring the characters and their cartoon world to life. With every turn of the page, and with every twist in the story, you will almost hear their voices come to life as well. Stay tuned . . . Soon, you actually will . . .

~ J.Z. Bingham

Once upon a time, in a village by the sea,
There lived a happy little dog and cat family.
Early one morning at the break of dawn,
They gathered outside on their tidy green lawn.

Their eyes were pointed high, up above them, in the sky.
They watched excitedly as the stork flew by.
As he circled in closer, they couldn't help but see,
His funny shirt, sandals, sunglasses, and goatee!
From his neck hung a pouch, dangling to and fro.
Little Sammy was inside, smiling wide; he seemed to glow.

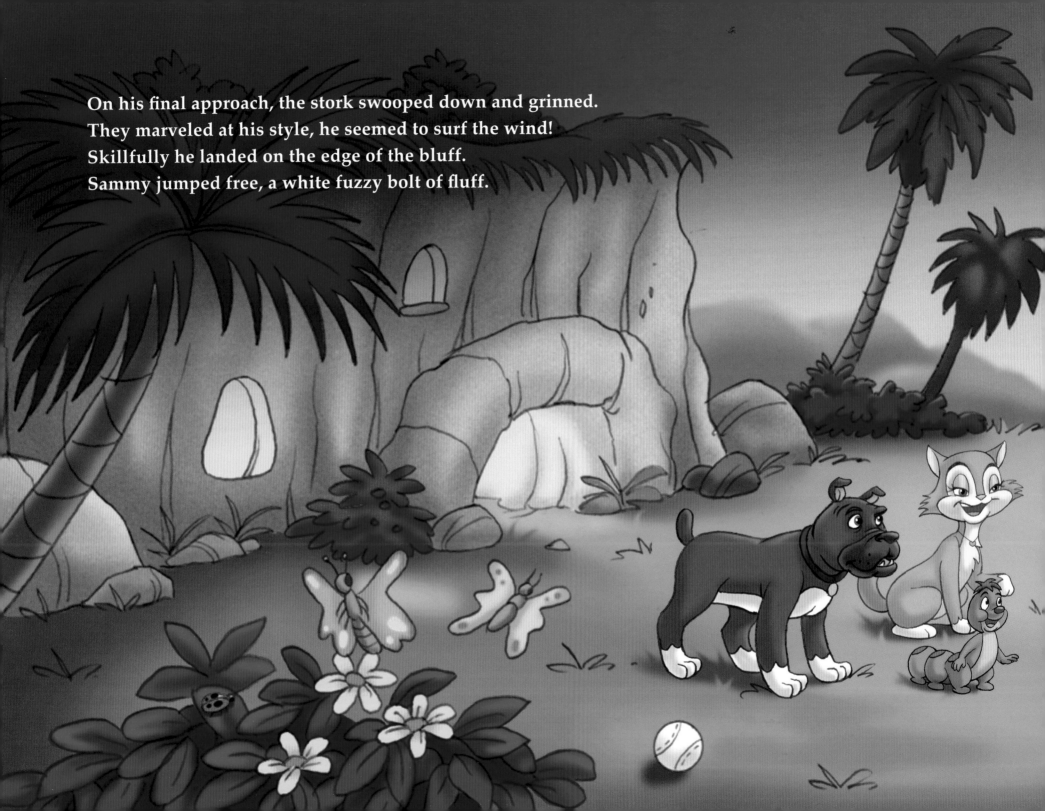

On his final approach, the stork swooped down and grinned.
They marveled at his style, he seemed to surf the wind!
Skillfully he landed on the edge of the bluff.
Sammy jumped free, a white fuzzy bolt of fluff.

"Here you go, M'am,
You're little Dude's got lots of spunk!
Was a blast getting here,
A high flyin' slam dunk!"

"My, my!" Dad exclaimed,
"What a ball of energy!"

"That he is!" Mom agreed,
"And just as cute as he can be!"

"Gotta fly," laughed the Stork, "My next delivery is due."

Sammy perked up, thinking he was going too.

"Sorry, little buddy, this is where
    I leave you."

He gathered up his pouch and
    flew off into the blue.

Sammy quickly fell into a nice routine.
His new neighborhood seemed so calm and serene.
As he sat there gazing out from his front window,
He started planning all the places he would go.

One of his very favorite things to do,
Became fetching mail from the carrier
          in blue . . .
Another highlight, he would find with
               great delight,
          Was the cat next door, always
               cheery and bright . . .

Sammy soon became famous; they all knew his name.
It seemed everywhere he went he had a claim to fame!

His sister stared in awe as his reputation grew;
Perched up high with her friends, they saw what he could do!

Now satisfied and tired, Sammy called it a day.
As he neared his front door, he heard his Dad loudly say,
"Sammy! Look at you! Now what have you done?
I think it's time for a talk, just father and son . . ."

Dad was trying to keep calm, but Sammy knew he was mad.
He seemed to tower over Sammy, "Um, okay Dad . . ."

"I know it must be fun, Son, to dig and explore,
But tearing up the neighborhood CAN'T HAPPEN ANYMORE!
Now march inside and clean your hide; it's time to learn some rules . . .
Causing trouble everywhere is just a life for fools!"

"Yes, Sir . . ." Sammy softly said with a frown.
He shuffled toward the door; now his spirits were down.
He saw his sister staring, through the window, with a smirk.
She winked at him and purred, "Sounds like an awful lot of work!"

Kat was watching closely,
but pretended not to hear.
She imagined "Prisoner Sammy"
and she grinned from ear to ear.

Ah yes! Sweet surrender . . .
all alone in his disgrace . . .
Locked up, while she takes
back her spot in 1st place!

After all had said "Goodnight,"
Sammy crawled into bed,
And soon a lovely plan
popped into his head.

He could stuff a pillow case
and sneak off early to the beach,
To quickly hide his stuff,
safe and sound, out of reach.
If he got up super early,
and beat everyone there,
Then no one would find out,
and he'd be free from care.

As Sammy softly snored,
Kat snuggled into her bed.
Dreams of days, filled with praise,
began to fill her head.

Back to number one!
What a beautiful scene:
Lounging on the beach,
catered to like a Queen!

Early in the morning, Sammy rose with the sun.
His pillow case was stuffed; to the beach he would run.
As he crossed the yard, Wiggleworm called out,
"Well, well, a little early to be up and about!"

"Sssh!" Sammy whispered, "Don't make such a huff!
I'm just going to the beach to drop off some stuff . . ."

"To the beach, so you say? Sounds like fun! Let's go!
If I have to stay here, I might let on you know . . ."

"You silly tattle-tale! Well . . . hurry up, let's go;
The whole gang will be there, and I don't want them to know!"

Off they went, down the path leading to the beach;
The surfers and the gulls already within reach.
They saw a little boat lying in the sand.
It seemed a safe place, but not what he had planned.

"You can leave your stuff here. Let's go for a run!
We'll come back later on . . . let's have some fun in the sun!"

Pretty soon, the gang arrived with beach towels and boards.
The surf was nice and strong. "Be sure to fasten your cords!"
Dutch was giving out instructions before their ride,
"Just try to tune in to the wave and glide!"

Sammy caught a curl and rode it all the way in!
"That a boy, Sammy! Let's see you do that again!"

Under the warm sun, his sister watched from her chair.
She caught herself smiling as Sammy caught some air.
By her feet, her friends were busy, building castles
    in the sand.
As she took in this whole scene, she thought,
    "Ah! Life is grand!"

Sammy ran up to his friends, his surfing lesson was now over.
"Those waves were pretty awesome!" He shook the water from his fur.
His sister rolled her eyes, as she dried off Sammy's spray.
The worm then yelled out, "You got some energy to play?"
"Sure, Wiggleworm! Climb on up! We'll run a while!"
So off they went for what became mile after mile.

After a few hours, Sammy ran out of gas.
As he slowed to a stop, Wiggleworm said, "What a BLAST!"
They plodded up the beach, and Sammy found the boat;
In it sat his sister, arms crossed, about to gloat.

"Sammy! What's all this? It looks like quite a stash!
If Mom and Dad found out, they just might ground you in a flash!"

"Aw, come on! Please don't tell! They're already mad at me!
I promise I'll be good!" Sammy cried with misery.

Seeing his sad eyes melted Kat just a bit.
"I'll tell you what," she said, "Take a rest right here and sit.
You look pretty tired. Here, I brought you a snack."

"You promise you won't tell when we all get back?"

"Don't worry, little brother, I'll stay on your side . . .
I just can't promise you that they won't tan your hide!"

"That's not funny!" yelled the worm. "Stop being mean to him!
He's just a little puppy . . . soon he'll learn to fit in!"

"Hey, I was only kidding! Gosh, golly, GEE WHIZ!
Don't get your legs tangled up, and your hair in a frizz!"
They had a little laugh and climbed inside for a snack.
They had to head home soon but didn't want to go back.

Silence settled in as clouds swallowed the sun.
A sleepy slumber overcame them, one by one.
The three little souls fell into dreamy repose.
Soon joined by a fourth, their friend the squirrel, Melrose.

As he jumped into the boat, he quickly realized,
To be very quiet, so they wouldn't be surprised.
Settling in next to Kat, he closed his eyes for a while.
The rerun of the day, in his mind, made him smile.

So now the souls asleep in the boat numbered four;
Unaware of the storm about to pound the shore.
The thunder claps were distant, dreamy drums in their heads.
The water rising under them, soft gliders on their beds.

The clouds grew big and dark; heavy drops
    were pouring down.
The stormy sea was surging; waves were
    crashing all around.
One by one, the four awoke to salty
    splashes of swells.
They tried to cry out, but the wind
    drowned out their yells.

Holding tight, full of fright, they rode
out the storm.
Until, finally, they saw what looked
like land taking form.
Up ahead, very faint, a rocky
mountaintop,
Was coming into view, as
the rain began to stop.

Inside the boat, all four were soaked, eyes wide with fright.
Up ahead they saw an island; what an eerie sight!

"What do we do now?"
"How do we get back home?"
"You think this island is deserted?"
"There's not much room to roam!"

Behind their boat, a shape appeared, real long and slow;
It was a whale, big and blue; it's eyes were mean and yellow!
It crept up silently and pushed their boat toward the shore.
Then quietly it swam away from them once more.

A glassy calm replaced the storm surrounding their boat.
The distant thunder struck a note, white-hot and remote.
An invisible magnet seemed to steer their course.
The island pulled them in with its dreamy force.

"Kat," Sammy whispered, "You know where we are?"
She seemed in a trance, "I know we've gone too far . . ."
The sun's rays warmed them as they glided toward the shore.
They made it through the storm; they reached land once more!

"We made it!" they cried out. All four were smiling wide!
They jumped free from the boat, thankful for low tide.
One by one, they ran around, kicking sand in the air.
Sammy did his Happy Dance without a care.

"Wow! That was rad! I never saw such a surf!"
"Yeah!" Melrose cried, "But I like land and turf!"
"I wasn't scared at all!" Wiggleworm declared.
"Hah!" Kat laughed out, "You were 'SCAREDER' than scared!"

Our crew of four were now dry and safe on the sand.
Together, they were ready to explore this new land.
They never would have dreamed they would sail away.
We never know what life may have in store for us today!

Salty Splashes

COLLECTION™

Salty Splashes

COLLECTION™